TO BOB AND COLLEEN

For reading early drafts of Stickler Loves the World *and*
offering comments, a big thanks to Bob Shea, Laurie Keller, Molly,
and of course my stickler of an editor, Maria Modugno —L.S.

STICKLER
loves the
WORLD

LANE SMITH

design by Molly Leach

RANDOM HOUSE STUDIO ⬛ NEW YORK

Many strange creatures lived in the
part of the forest where shadow met tree.

But the strangest of all was *Stickler*.

"Three new sticks!
A brown one, another brown one, and another brown one,"
said Stickler. "Why, even Crow will be impressed.

And he's seen it all!"

STICKS. Stickler loved them more than anything.

Except maybe . . .

"Fluffy cloud!

Pretty bat!

Sticky honey

Mushy moss!

Craggy stone!

Everything else.

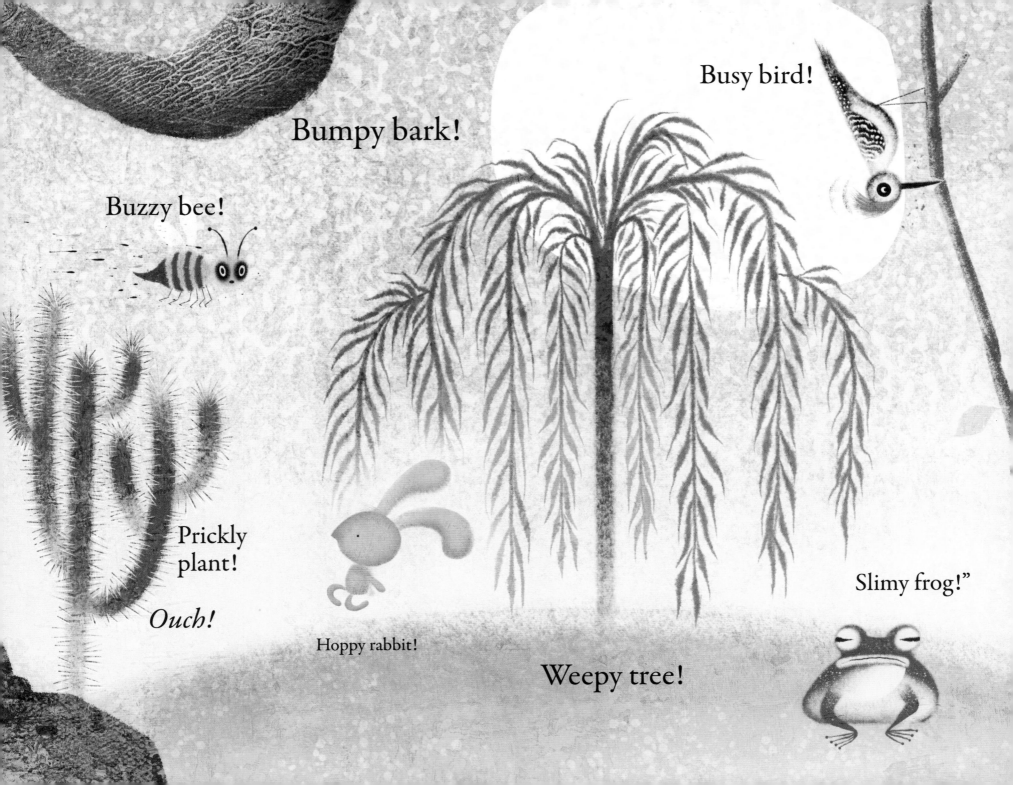

"If you think about it,
   our world has some pretty weird stuff in it!"
said Stickler, opening all eight of its eyes.

"Oh, to see it all anew.
   Wouldn't that be amazing?"

"Elpppp!" said a voice.

"Elp to *you,* stranger," said Stickler.

"I can see by your cutting-edge space helmet you are not from our Earth."

"Geh thii ovv ma *hedd*!"

"I do not understand your language, visitor-with-only-three-eyes,
but let me share with you the wonders of my planet."

"The morning SUN reaches through clouds.

Shake hands, it says. *Pleased to meet you!*"

"Colors bursting
like fireworks!

FLOWERS!

Look!
Puffballs! And tomorrow
there will be twice as many!"

Smell one.

Mmmmmmmmmmmmmmmmmmmm.

"Over here!

WAVES wave.

Hello!

Hello!

Goodbye!

Goodbye

"Feel it?

Wait for it.

There!

Did you feel it that time?

No?

It's like a whisper . . . but one you *feel*.

There it is again.

WIND."

"Behold!
The joy of ROCKS."

"And just think of the wonders we must pass **every day** without even **noticing**."

"Then there are THESE THINGS
dancing for us, falling, spinning, whirling, twirling, around and around!"

"Dizzzeeeee . . ."

"Crow, it's you!"
"I didn't think that can was ever coming off!
Thanks, Stickler, for opening my eyes."

"But, Crow,
      everything today . . .
      you've seen it all before."

"No, Stickler.
Today you really
did open my eyes."

POP!

"Crow, look. STARS for wishing.
Let us say our favorite wishes together."

"*Friendship! Happiness! World peace! Maple syrup!*"

"Zooks!" said Stickler, almost forgetting its most *favorite* thing of all. . . .

"Sticks!

Each one unique.

A brown one!

Another brown one!

Another brown one!

Another brown one

Wonders!"

With sticks in hand and wing,
the two friends walked home.
QUIETLY.

"Because," whispered Stickler,
"no words can truly describe a world
so amazing,
so weird,
so wonderful."

But Stickler tried anyway.

"Chirpy crickets! Misty fog! Shiny moon! Glowy fireflies! Fuzzy moths! Hooty owl! Dewy grass!"